# HOLI AROUND THE WORLD

By Jeff Sferazza

Gareth Stevens
PUBLISHING

Library of Congress Cataloging-in-Publication Data

Names: Sferazza, Jeff, author.
Title: Holidays around the world / Jeff Sferazza.
Description: New York : Gareth Stevens Publishing, 2019. | Series: Adventures in culture | Includes bibliographical references and index.
Identifiers: LCCN 2018000112| ISBN 9781538218679 (library bound) | ISBN 9781538218693 (pbk.) | ISBN 9781538218709 (6 pack)
Subjects: LCSH: Holidays–Juvenile literature.
Classification: LCC GT3933 .S44 2019 | DDC 394.26–dc23
LC record available at https://lccn.loc.gov/2018000112

Published in 2019 by
**Gareth Stevens Publishing**
111 East 14th Street, Suite 349
New York, NY 10003

Designer: Katelyn E. Reynolds
Editor: Meta Manchester

Photo credits: Cover, p. 1 wong yu liang/Shutterstock.com; pp. 2-24 (background texture) Flas100/Shutterstock.com; p. 5 Monkey Business Images/Shutterstock.com; p. 7 flydragon/Shutterstock.com; p. 9 India Picture/Shutterstock.com; p. 11 kiraziku2u/Shutterstock.com; p. 13 SVEN NACKSTRAND/AFP/Getty Images; p. 15 CRISTINA ALDEHUELA/AFP/Getty Images; p. 17 Alexandre Dimou/Icon Sport via Getty Images; p. 19 Wollertz/Shutterstock.com; p. 21 dr.ted/Shutterstock.com.

Printed in the United States of America

CPSIA compliance information: Batch #CS18GS: For further information contact Gareth Stevens, New York, New York at 1-800-542-2595.

# CONTENTS

**Boldface** words appear in the glossary.

# Hooray for Holidays!

Think of your favorite holiday. You might love it because you get to dress up, open gifts, or stay home from school. People around the world **celebrate** many different holidays. You might want to start celebrating a new special day, too!

4

# Songkran

In Thailand, people celebrate Songkran (SONG-krahn) each April. This is a **festival** for the Thai New Year. To celebrate, people throw water on each other. It's supposed to wash away bad luck, but it looks like a water fight!

# Diwali

Diwali (dee-VAH-lee) is a holiday in India, but it's celebrated by **Hindus** everywhere. It's called the Festival of Lights. Lamps light up houses. Some are placed in rivers. The lights welcome the goddess of good luck.

# Eid al-Fitr

For 1 month each year, **Muslims** fast. That means they don't eat or drink during the day. At the end of the month, they celebrate Eid al-Fitr (EED uhl-FIHT-ruh), or the "Feast of Fast-Breaking." People wear new clothes and eat special meals.

# Midsummer's Eve

Midsummer's Eve is a holiday in June that celebrates the longest day of the year. In some parts of the Northern **Hemisphere**, the sun never sets! In Sweden, people sing and dance around a pole **decorated** with flowers and other plants.

# Midsummer's Eve in Sweden

13

# Aboakyer Festival

Each May, the Aboakyer (uh-BAW-chay) festival is celebrated in Ghana, a country in Africa. It's a time to remember how the people of Winneba traveled to Ghana long ago. There's a hunt in which people catch a live antelope with nothing but their bare hands!

15

# Boxing Day

Boxing Day is celebrated in Great Britain, Canada, Australia, New Zealand, and other countries. It's the first weekday after Christmas. It was once a day when people gave gifts in boxes to the poor. Today, it's a day for sports and shopping.

a **rugby** match on Boxing Day

# Independence Day

Five nations in Central America celebrate Independence Day on September 15. El Salvador, Guatemala, Costa Rica, Honduras, and Nicaragua **declared** themselves free of Spanish control on September 15, 1821. Parades are a big part of the celebration.

Independence Day in Costa Rica

## Chuseok

Chuseok (CHOO-sawk) is a fall holiday in Korea. It's also known as the Harvest Moon Festival. People eat a meal together. They also offer food to **ancestors**. Would you like to celebrate one of the holidays in this book?

food for Chuseok

21

# GLOSSARY

**ancestor:** a family member who lived long before you

**celebrate:** to honor with special activities

**declare:** to say or state something in a public way

**decorate:** to make something look nice by adding extra items to it

**festival:** a special time or event when people gather to celebrate

**hemisphere:** one-half of Earth

**Hindu:** a follower of a major religion in India

**Muslim:** a follower of the religion of Islam

**rugby:** a football-like sport popular in Great Britain, Australia, and New Zealand

# FOR MORE INFORMATION

## BOOKS

Carpentiere, Elizabeth Crooker. *Festivals Around the World.* Peterborough, NH: Cobblestone Publishing Company, 2017.

Ingalls, Ann. *Christmas Traditions Around the World.* Mankato, MN: Child's World, 2013.

Lehman-Wilzig, Tami, and Vicki Wehrman. *Hanukkah Around the World.* Minneapolis, MN: Kar-Ben, 2011.

## WEBSITES

**9 Winter Holidays Around the World**
*www.learningliftoff.com/9-winter-holidays-around-the-world/*
Read about some well-known and not-so-familiar winter holidays.

**Holidays**
*www.ducksters.com/holidays/kids_calendar.php*
Holidays are listed by month on this site.

# INDEX